FRANCESCO TIRELLI'S ICE CREAM SHOP

In memory of my beloved father-in-law, Prof. Isaac Mayer 1927—2018, who took advantage of the gift of life he gained in order to make the world a better place.

—T.M.

KAR-BEN PUBLISHING, INC.
A division of Lerner Publishing Group, Inc.
241 First Avenue North
Minneapolis, MN 55401 USA
1-800-4-KARBEN

Website address: www.karben.com

Main body text set in Veronika LT Std 13/16
Typeface provided by Linotype AG

Library of Congress Cataloging-in-Publication Data

Names: Meir, Tamar, 1976– author. | Albert, Yael, illustrator. | Applebaum, Noga, translator.
Title: Francesco Tirelli's ice cream shop / Tamar Meir ; illustrated by Yael Albert ; English translation by Noga Applebaum.
Other titles: Hanut ha-gelidah Ferantsesko Tireli. English
Description: Minneapolis : Kar-Ben Publishing, [2019] | Series: Holocaust | Summary: One winter in Budapest during the Second World War, an Italian closes his ice cream shop for the season, using the storefront to hide his Jewish friends and neighbors, including a boy named Peter. Based on a true story.
Identifiers: LCCN 2018033629| ISBN 9781541534650 (lb : alk. paper) | ISBN 9781541534742 (pb : alk. paper)
Subjects: LCSH: World War, 1939–1945—Jews—Rescue—Juvenile fiction. | World War, 1939–1945—Hungary—Juvenile fiction. | CYAC: World War, 1939–1945—Jews—Rescue—Fiction. | World War, 1939–1945—Hungary—Fiction. | Ice cream parlors—Fiction. | Holocaust, Jewish (1939–1945)—Hungary—Fiction. | Budapest (Hungary)—History—1872-1945—Fiction. | Hungary—History—1918-1945—Fiction.
Classification: LCC PZ7.1.M4687 Fr 2019 | DDC [E]—dc23

LC record available at https://lccn.loc.gov/2018033629

Manufactured in the United States of America
2-48385-35731-9/12/2019

FRANCESCO TIRELLI'S ICE CREAM SHOP

Tamar Meir

illustrated by Yael Albert

translated by Noga Applebaum

KAR-BEN
PUBLISHING

Francesco Tirelli loved ice cream so much that at least once a day he would find an excuse to pass by Carlo Tirelli's ice cream cart. Uncle Carlo was very fond of his nephew. Every time Francesco paid him a visit, Uncle Carlo would give him a small pinch on his right cheek, a big kiss on his left cheek, and lift him up in the air, so high that Francesco could see all the ice cream flavors on the cart below.

Then his uncle would put Francesco down and ask,

"Hazelnut or berry?
　　Cinnamon or cherry?
　　　　Coffee or toffee?"

And Francesco, with a tiny smile, would always reply,

"I love them all."

So it went, nearly every day.

One day his mother, Emma, told him, "Enough! You will end up growing a *gelateria* in your tummy!"

Francesco gazed at her silently. Paused. Then grinned.

Francesco continued to love ice cream,
    even when he was no longer a small child,
        and even when he was no longer an older child,
            and even when he was all grown up.

He continued loving ice cream just as much when he
left Italy and moved away, to a country named Hungary.
But nowhere in the capital city of Budapest could he
find ice cream as good as his uncle's.

"What a shame," he thought to himself, "that I didn't end up growing a *gelateria* in my tummy, just as my mother said, then I would have been able to eat the ice cream I love anywhere in the world."

He thought about ice cream so much that one day, instead of growing a *gelateria* in his tummy, Francesco grew a *gelateria* in his mind. Francesco knew that if he didn't open an ice cream shop soon, he would never be able to get it out of his head.

"An ice cream shop?" everyone said.

"In Budapest?
      This isn't Italy.
           This isn't Rome.
                This isn't Venice.
                    This isn't Florence.

This is Budapest. Here you can open a *Palacsinta* shop, or a *Körözött* shop, a *Zserbó* cake shop, a shop selling *Rakott Krumpli*, or stuffed *Gombóc*, or *Kürtöškalács*.

But ice cream? Who will buy your ice cream?"

But Francesco Tirelli would not give up.

He opened an ice cream shop right in the center of Budapest. He sold ice cream and chocolate to everyone, even to those who said nobody would buy it.

Francesco thought to himself, "Mothers are always right. I did end up with an ice cream shop growing in my tummy (and my head), just like my mother said."

One child in Budapest who loved ice cream was Peter. Every day he would find an excuse to pass by Francesco Tirelli's shop. Sometimes he would buy ice cream, sometimes he would just walk in, sometimes he would just peep through the window. Francesco would look at him from inside the shop, smile, and wink at him with his left eye.

More than anything, Peter loved hearing Francesco ask,

"Hazelnut or berry?
    Cinnamon or cherry?
        Coffee or toffee?"

And Peter, with a tiny smile, would reply,
"I love them all."

When Francesco heard this reply, he would grin, and serve Peter an extra-large scoop.

One day, Peter's mother, Lilly, told him,
"Enough! You will end up living in an ice cream shop!"
Peter gazed at her silently. Paused. Then smiled a tiny smile.

Years went by.

Peter was no longer a child, he was a teenager, and the city of Budapest had also changed.

The people were not as happy. There was a war, and everyone was afraid.

Even Peter didn't feel like buying ice cream. He would just stop and look at the shop every time he passed by.

One cold winter day, Peter saw Francesco closing the shop.
Peter said to Francesco, "Maybe by summer things will be different,
and people will buy ice cream again." They smiled sadly at each other.

Francesco hated the war. He was also a little anxious.

What would happen to Hungary, and Italy, and to all the people he knew and cared about? But he was less afraid than some of his neighbors. He was Italian, and people in Hungary liked Italians.

Peter's family was very afraid. They were Jewish, and in Hungary, as in neighboring Germany, they were no longer wanted, even though they had harmed nobody. Peter's parents discussed it. They decided to hide for a while. Maybe by summer everything will be different and the war will end.

But where could they hide? Who would help them?

Francesco Tirelli was also thinking.

"I'm Italian. I don't need to be afraid. The Hungarians like me.
But what will happen to my neighbors? What will happen to
Peter's family? What will happen to other children's families?

Someone has to offer them shelter,
to help them hide.

Someone . . . I've got it!
My ice cream shop!
I will help them.
I am that someone!

It's winter. Winter is cold.
In the winter I don't sell ice cream."

Francesco cautiously consulted his friends,
and they all said,
"Hide Jews? In an Ice cream shop?
It's too risky we fear, and besides it's clear
They are not our kin, they are not from here."
Francesco gazed at them silently.
Paused, and said nothing.
He just smiled a sad smile.

But secretly,
without telling anyone,
he started inviting Jewish people to his shop,
and even found them other hiding places.

Plans he laid,
arrangements he made.
Though he was afraid
he secretly paid
to have notes delivered, offering aid.
Peter's parents received such a note.
On it was scribbled an address:
No. 7 Lövölde Tér.
They immediately understood.
This address had distinct aromas
of cinnamon and cherry,
toffee and coffee,
and all the rest.
Slowly Jewish people
gathered in the shop:
Peter and his parents came,
neighbors from across the street came,
and friends from synagogue came.
A girl called Hannah and her mother
also came.
Before the war they used to buy
a lot of strawberry ice cream
from the shop.

More and more people came. Francesco took care of them all. He brought them food to eat, and water to drink, and even a newspaper so they would know what was happening in the world outside.

"Thank you!" said the people, moved by his kindness.
"Thank you!" said Peter's parents.

Peter thought to himself, "I did end up living in an ice cream shop, just like my mother said I would."

Francesco gazed at them silently, and smiled.
He was delighted to be able to help.

For many days, Peter, his parents, and all the others stayed hidden in the back room of Francesco Tirelli's closed ice cream shop. Outside the snow was falling, outside the rain was pouring, outside the war was raging, but inside the shop people were safe.

The days passed, and suddenly it was the month of Kislev, and the festival of Hanukkah was approaching. The people in the shop were sad.

"It's Hanukkah," they said, "but we are not at home. We are not celebrating the light. We are hidden in darkness."

The neighbor from across the street said, "Maybe we should try? Maybe we can find a way to light Hanukkah candles?"

Hannah looked up hopefully. A friend from the synagogue remembered that he'd seen a bottle of cooking oil somewhere.

Peter longed for them to succeed, for someone to find a hanukkiah, for someone to..."I will be that someone!" he decided. "I will find a hanukkiah!"

But where? Venturing out is dangerous. In the shop there are cups and spoons, there is a refrigerator, there are small bottles with tantalizing aromas, but there is no hanukkiah.

Peter entered the shop. He checked the back room. He sought and searched, tried and rummaged, looked right, and left, and right again.

And then he saw it. A hanukkiah? No! A mold for making chocolate. Melted chocolate could be poured into the mold, and taken out when it hardened.

Peter looked at the mold, and smelled the delicious aroma of chocolate. He could almost taste it on the tip of his tongue. It had been so long since he had chocolate, or chocolate-flavored ice cream.

But the mold had no chocolate in it, just empty holes. He counted them. He counted again. He couldn't believe it. The mold had exactly eight holes. Someone remembered seeing a bottle of cooking oil. There it was, on a shelf.

And so, that year, inside an ice cream shop, in the heart of cold, dark Budapest, a chocolate hanukkiah burned brightly. And everyone hoped and prayed that by summer everything would be different.

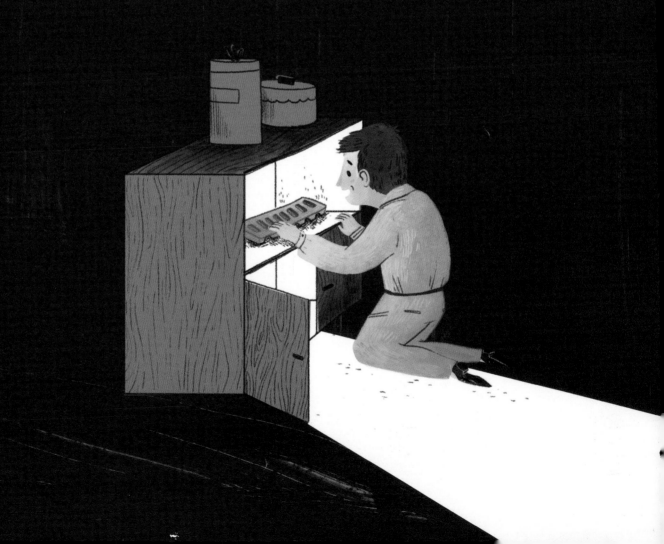

Winter passed, and in the spring the war was over.

Peter, Hannah, and their families, the neighbors from across the street, and all the other people who were with them in the shop gradually tried to return to their normal lives.

Francesco reopened his ice cream shop, and continued to sell ice cream in the flavors he loved so much.

Hazelnut and berry.
Cinnamon and cherry.
Coffee and toffee.
In all sizes, to people of all kinds.

Francesco knew that what he had achieved was bigger and sweeter than any ice cream scoop he had ever sold or eaten in his life.

Peter grew up and moved to Israel.

He studied, and then taught at a university.
He never forgot Francesco. And he never forgot
how important it is to help those in need.

He married Sarah, and had children,
grandchildren, and great-grandchildren.
And they all loved ice cream.

Best of all they loved going to the ice
cream shop in Jerusalem with Grandpa
Isaac, who once lived in Budapest,
and was called Peter.

Epilogue

The Second World War took place during the years 1939-1945. Germany, ruled by the Nazi party, conquered many countries all across Europe. In each of these countries, the Nazis hunted down the Jews, and perpetrated the genocide that is known as the Holocaust.

Many Jews tried to escape and find somewhere to hide. Fortunately for them, along with the cruelty of the war years there were also some good people, brave and noble non-Jews, who at great risk to themselves were prepared to help the fugitives. These people are called "Righteous among the Nations."

One of them was Francesco Tirelli.

Francesco Tirelli was born in Italy in 1898, but worked in Budapest, Hungary. In 1944, after the Nazis invaded Hungary, Tirelli aided Jews locating hideouts for them. Some hid in the back room of his ice cream shop. In 2008, following appeals made by Isaac (Peter) Mayer, Francesco Tirelli was recognized as one of the Righteous among the Nations.

Professor Isaac (Peter) Mayer was born in 1927 in Budapest, Hungary. In 1944 he hid with fellow Jews in a village outside Budapest, but later escaped back to Budapest. There he joined his parents, Chaim and Lilly (Golda) and together with some fifteen other Jews, they took shelter in Tirelli's ice cream shop.

The father, Chaim, passed away shortly after the war ended. Isaac immigrated to Israel, and later he was joined by his mother Lilly. In Israel he became a chemistry Professor at the Hebrew University in Jerusalem. He married Sarah, and the two had children, grandchildren and great grandchildren.

The author is his daughter-in-law.

Isaac (Peter) Mayer and his wife, Sarah, by the site of the ice cream shop in Budapest.

Isaac (Peter) Mayer and his wife Sarah in Israel, 1958.